For those who have blessed my life—Micheal, Lois, Wayne,
Adam and Angie, Rebecca and Eric,
and especially for Hannah Rebecca, Blake Adam,
and all my future grandbabies.

Cynda

For Nana, here is Angel #74. With love and prayers—

"Shirley"

Published 2007 by Concordia Publishing House
3558 S. Jefferson Avenue
St. Louis, MO 63118-3968
1-800-325-3040 • www.cph.org

Manufactured in China

1   2   3   4   5   6   7   8   9   10   16   15   14   13   12   11   10   09   08   07

Where Do Angels Sleep?

By Cynda Strong

Illustrated by Julia Denos

CONCORDIA PUBLISHING HOUSE • SAINT LOUIS

Angels circle 'round me
When I slumber
through the night.

They keep me safe
throughout the day
From dawn 'til
evening light.

They circle o'er me when I play;
They hover 'round my bed.

But where do angels go to rest
To lay a weary head?

Surely angels need some time
To play, to sleep, to eat,

To visit Jesus on His throne,
To kneel at Jesus' feet.

My mom said something curious—
That angels never rest,

And guarding Jesus' children
Is the job that they like best!

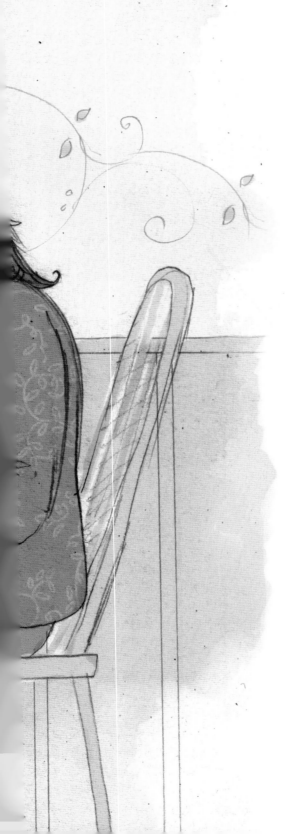

They have no need
of food or rest;
They want to please the Lord.

And so they stay around us,
According to His Word.

I know that Jesus saves me,
Forgives my sins with love.